THE PACKAGE
IN HYPERSPACE

THE
PACKAGE
IN
HYPERSPACE

Janet Asimov

Illustrations by
John Gampert

Walker and Company
New York

First published in the United States of America
in 1988 by the Walker Publishing Company, Inc.

Published simultaneously in Canada by Thomas Allen & Son
Canada, Limited, Markham, Ontario.

LIBRARY OF CONGRESS

Library of Congress Cataloging-in-Publication Data

Asimov, Janet.
   The package in hyperspace / Janet Jeppson Asimov.
      p.   cm.
   Summary: Twelve-year-old Ginnela and her younger brother Pete find
themselves trapped on a disabled spaceship and must figure out how to survive.
   ISBN 0-8027-6823-7 (lib. bdg.). ISBN 0-8027-6822-9
   [1. Science fiction.] I. Title.
PZ7.A836Pac   1988   [Fic]—dc19   88-4984

Printed in the United States of America

10 9 8 7 6 5 4 3 2 1

Book design by Laurie McBarnette
Text illustrations by John Gampert

Books by Janet Asimov:

Norby, the Mixed-Up Robot
Norby's Other Secret
Norby and the Lost Princess
Norby and the Invaders
Norby and the Queen's Necklace
Norby Finds a Villain
How to Enjoy Writing
(all with Isaac Asimov)

Mind Transfer
The Package in Hyperspace

Laughing Space (with Isaac Asimov)
The Second Experiment
The Last Immortal
The Mysterious Cure
(as J. O. Jeppson)

For Maureen,
who has a younger brother
and also copes with mine.

THE PACKAGE
IN HYPERSPACE

CHAPTER

1

CRASH!

"What was *that!*" Ginnela Wayd's legs suddenly felt shaky beneath her and she sat down on her suitcase. The transporter room of Fedcargo Samson seemed to be vibrating like the inside of a drum, and her stomach was doing the same. Then she remembered she was twelve and in charge of Pete, so she made room for him to sit on the suitcase too.

"Getting out of hyperspace never felt this horrible before," said her little brother. In the travel cage beside him, his pet loffo wailed and began clawing at the door.

The ten other passengers on the huge freighter, waiting in line to transport to the planet Merkina, scowled and grumbled about the roughness of reentry into normal space.

"No excuse for it," said an elderly woman. "A ship that carries any passengers at all should make smoother hyperjumps."

"Will we be delayed?" asked a fat man with a briefcase.

With a triumphant screech, the loffo pushed open the door of his cage and galloped on all six legs into the passenger corridor, his pink fur standing on end. Pete ran after him.

"I'll be right back, Ginn," shouted Pete. "Don't transport to Merkina without me."

Ginnela moved her suitcase out of line. "Does anybody know what happened? I think something hit the ship before the Samson left hyperspace."

"Nonsense!" said an elderly man. "Collisions in hyperspace are supposed to be impossible."

"We crashed into something," said Ginnela stubbornly.

Just then the young officer stationed at the transporter controls looked up from the computer monitor, his face pale. "All passengers prepare to transport at once."

"But what happened to the ship?" asked the elderly man.

"No time to explain," replied the officer, his voice anxious.

At that moment loud electronic bells began to sound through the Samson's loudspeakers, making conversation difficult. The passengers picked up their luggage and grouped together on the transporter plate.

Ginnela shrank back against the wall of the transporter room, in the shadow of a large crate that would be the first of the cargo to go to the planet Merkina. She watched the transporter officer and saw that he was much too frightened to count how many passengers were on the plate.

He touched a switch, and ten, not twelve, passengers vanished, their molecular patterns sent at light speed to a similar transporter plate on Merkina.

Pete must be having trouble with Lof, thought Ginnela. She wished the bells would stop.

Suddenly there was silence, and then the loudspeaker blared out again. It was Captain Velsky's voice.

"Abandon ship! All crew abandon ship at once."

The men and women of the Samson's crew ran down the ramp from the crew's quarters and clustered on the trans-

2

porter plate. They all looked frightened, and Ginnela could hear the words "crash" and "overload" as they talked excitedly together.

The transporter officer touched the controls again, and again everyone on the plate disappeared, just as Captain Velsky rushed in pulling the Samson's Chief Engineer.

"Let me go!" shouted the Chief. "I tell you, after the collision we should have aborted the hyperjump. . . ."

"Impossible with the main computer out," said Velsky. "Get on the plate."

"No—I might be able to save my engines from overload."

"Get on, blast you," shouted Velsky, struggling with the Chief. "It's too late. One engine is already destroyed and the other is on overload, and there's nothing we can do about it." He motioned to the transporter officer, who left the control board and came to the assistance of the Captain. He held the Chief tightly.

"Let me go," cried the Chief. "I'd rather die with the Samson than not even try . . ."

Captain Velsky strode to the transporter controls. "Hold onto the Chief. I'll operate the transporter and preset the controls so I can go after you. Stay on the plate!"

The Chief, still held by the young transporter officer, went to Merkina under protest. Velsky sighed and preset the controls carefully.

Ginnela moved out of the shadow.

"Miss Wayd! Why are you still here?"

"My brother had to go after his pet loffo. I don't know what's taking him so long."

"The kid that keeps talking about being an orphan?"

"Yes," said Ginnela, embarrassed. She could never stop Pete from telling everyone that they were orphans. "He should be here soon. He's only nine, but he's smart and reliable." She didn't add that the loffo was neither.

4

Velsky grunted and said, "Bridge computer, are you still operating?"

"Yes, Captain."

"Inside scanners still functional?"

"In this half of the ship, Captain."

"Locate Petevus Wayd."

"Yes, Captain." In a moment, the holoscreen monitor showed a thin, red-headed boy standing on top of a big black chair in a strange room full of blinking control panels. He seemed to be trying to unhook the elongated, pink-furred shape of a loffo from an open ventilation outlet in the ceiling.

"Blast the boy," muttered Velsky. "How did he get to the control room? Up through the dining salon, I suppose, although that door's supposed to be locked on the passenger side."

"He doesn't mean any harm," said Ginnela. "He's just very fond of his loffo."

"Petevus Wayd, come to the transporter room at once!"

"Soon as I get Lof down," said Pete, and stepped back too far. Ginnela screamed as she saw him fall to the control room floor with a thump. He rolled out of sight behind the Captain's chair and did not reappear.

"Great galaxy!" said Velsky. "I'll get him, but I'm not taking chances with either of you. Step onto the transporter plate now, Miss Wayd. It's not safe to stay here. You'll have to wait for your brother on Merkina."

He picked up Ginnela and put her on the transporter plate, but she sagged, as if she could not stand up.

"What's the matter?" asked Velsky. "Don't faint, now."

"Oh, Captain, I'm so scared. I'm only twelve and do I have to go alone?"

"Everyone else is safe on Merkina. Stand up or sit down on the plate, and I'll go back to the controls . . ."

She straightened up so suddenly that the Captain was thrown off balance. Then Ginnela kicked his feet from under him and ran to the transporter controls before he could move.

"Stop!" yelled Velsky, but she had already touched the preset switch. Ginnela noticed that as the Captain vanished, his face showed a mixture of guilt and relief.

She studied the control panel for a moment, to memorize how the controls were set for transporting to Merkina. In the monitor, she could see Lof frantically leaping from the Captain's chair to the other side, where Pete must still be. Was Pete dead?

Ginnela ran into the main passenger corridor that led out of the transporter room, at the stern of this half of the Samson, toward the curved bow where the dining salon was just under the control room, once called the Captain's bridge in old-time ocean ships on planet Earth.

The dining salon's other door, to the kitchens and from there to the crew's quarters and the control room, was locked, after all. Ginnela remembered that she could get to the crew's quarters from the transporter room and, angry with herself for not having thought of that in the first place, went back through the passenger corridor toward the stern.

It wasn't, of course, the real stern of the ship, for the Samson was shaped like a big egg that had a short-stemmed, fat lollipop stuck into the blunt end. The control room was at the pointy end of the egg, with the crew cabins behind it, the passenger cabins and dining salon below, and the ship's hold underneath everything else. The stern "lollipop" contained the two drive engines with the main computer between them.

As Ginnela ran, her footsteps sounded too loud over the soft hum of the ship. The ship was still working or the hum wouldn't be there. Why had the Captain been in such a hurry? What was the danger?

Ginnela remembered the word "overload." What did it mean?

She had almost reached the transporter room when the ship roared like an erupting volcano and she was thrown down. In a few seconds a tremendous wind began pushing her to the open door of the transporter room.

Forgetting that she had been trying to reach the transporter room, she fought against the wind, gripping the wall rail until her hands ached.

There was a hideous screech of tearing metal, and she saw, through the open door, a pointed, silvery shape piercing the back wall of the transporter room. It was moving toward her, twisting as it came, and out of a black opening in it poured multicolored boxes, whirling in the wind.

The silvery shape did not completely fill the gash it had made in the Samson's hull. Ginnela could see the multicolored boxes dancing out into the black of space.

"Please, ship, shut this door!" she shouted. "The air is leaving the ship! Please shut the door!"

CHAPTER

LOST

The clasp holding Ginnela's long, straight brown hair in a ponytail snapped open in the wind and fell to the floor. She didn't dare let go with one hand to push back her hair, so she peered through it, trying to see how fast the silver thing was coming at her.

"Oh, no!" The Wayds' suitcase whirled around with the boxes and headed toward the hole in the Samson's hull. She lost sight of it because the silver object got in the way, coming to a halt three-quarters of the way into the transporter room with a final scream of metal on metal.

The horror was not over. The wind was still too strong for her to back away from the deadly open door to the transporter room. The silver object didn't plug the hole in the Samson's hull completely. Beyond the jagged edges was the black of outer space.

Suddenly the silver point began to glow a brilliant yellow, and in another second flared to deep orange. "Don't shoot at me!" she shouted, her words lost in the roar of escaping air.

The very tip of the orange point sparked red. Ginnela winced, expecting to feel terrible pain, but instead her stomach lurched. It was a familiar sensation.

Through the crack in the hull, the black of outer space changed to a fuzzy gray, and at that moment, an emergency panel slid across the corridor. The noise stopped, for air was no longer rushing past Ginnela.

There was also no way to get into the transporter room from the passenger corridor where she was. She could not go to the crew's quarters from the transporter room, as she had intended. Pushing her hair out of her face, she didn't stop to pick up the clasp, but hurried back to the dining salon.

"Pete!" she yelled, pounding on the door to the kitchen. There was no answer, and there was no other way to go up to the control room.

But there had to be, or how else could Pete have got there? Lof must have run through the passenger corridor and, finding their cabin door shut, run on looking for a place to hide. Loffos always did when they were frightened. They looked for tunnels, preferably high up like the ones they dug in the tall cliffs of their native planet.

High up? Ginnela looked at one of the drapes beside the fake window (a holoscreen that could show the same forward view of outer space that was shown to the control room above). The drape was torn slightly, halfway up. She walked over to it and pulled it aside.

Behind the drape was the opening of a ventilation duct, and the screen had been broken open. In addition to two tiny, manipulative tentacles on top of each forward paw, loffos had strong digging claws in their four other feet. Lof must have been determined to find a safe place.

Ginnela climbed up the drape and managed to squeeze into the duct opening. For once she was grateful that she

9

was undersized and skinny for twelve. Even so, she had to crawl on her stomach through the duct.

The duct ended above a kitchen table that held a newly made apple pie, still warm from the oven. There was a hole in the pie, and a small chunk was missing. Lof was a vegetarian but didn't like warm food, so Pete must have been unable to resist grabbing a handful of pie to eat on the chase.

Ginnela swung down and went directly to the open door at the other side of the room. It led to a ramp that went up to the crew's corridor, and that took her directly to the control room, where Pete was now sitting in the Captain's chair, patting Lof.

"Hello, Ginn. Sorry it took so long to capture Lof. I'm afraid I slipped and knocked the wind out of myself, but I think I'm all right now." He cradled Lof in his arms. "I did feel awful woozy a few minutes ago, though."

"It felt that way when we entered hyperspace the first time, so I think that was the Samson going *back* into hyperspace. Besides, I saw the gray of it outside the damaged hull."

"But we're not supposed to go back into hyperspace. We're at the transporter coordinates for Merkina."

"Let's go to our cabin, Pete. I'll explain." Ginnela led him back to the kitchen, unlatched the door to the dining salon so they wouldn't be locked out of the kitchen again, and walked down the passenger corridor to their cabin, thinking hard all the way.

"Ginn, there's a blank wall at the end of the corridor. Isn't there supposed to be a door to the transporter room?"

She went into their cabin and sat on her bunk. Pete sat on his, and Lof lay beside him, warbling happily as if nothing could possibly be wrong now that the ship wasn't lurching.

"We'll be late transporting down to Merkina," said Pete.

11

"Uncle Roy might be angry and I thought we were going to try to make a good impression. . . ."

"I think we're going to be very late. I think we're stuck here. I mean, the ship is. . . ."

"Where is here?"

"I don't know. Hyperspace doesn't have any dimensions, just imaginary coordinates ships can jump to and then jump out into normal space. We're back in hyperspace, and I don't know if we've traveled in it or stayed still or what. And I don't know how long we'll be here."

Pete shrugged. "Let's go back and eat that apple pie."

"You idiot! You're supposed to be so smart, and you haven't even noticed that there wasn't anybody in the control room or the kitchen or anywhere! There's nobody on the ship but you and me—and that silly pet of yours that got us in this fix in the first place!"

"We're all alone?"

"Everybody else transported to Merkina while the ship was in normal space. Captain Velsky said it was an emergency, and even the crew had to abandon ship because the main computer and one of the drive engines were knocked out, and the other drive engine was overloading."

"But why?"

Ginnela leaned back on her bunk, hoping she wouldn't cry. "Captain Velsky didn't explain, but I think I know. Just as the Samson was about to go out of hyperspace into normal space, another ship, much smaller than ours, rammed into us. Right into the back . . ."

"The stern," said Pete. "All the way back, into the engine section?"

"It must have, if it knocked out the main computer and one of the drive engines. When the second drive engine blew up with that awful roar, the explosion must have shoved the other ship forward, right into the transporter

12

room. I saw it, stuck into our ship, the air leaking out of the broken hull of the transporter room. I might have been shot out into space, too, but I saw the black of space change to the gray of hyperspace, and then an emergency panel sealed off the corridor."

Pete was silent for a moment, while Lof, tuning into the anxiety of the humans, began to moan gently, his upturned nose wobbling. The first pair of his six legs patted Pete's thigh. Lof always seemed to believe that sympathetic moans and soft pats would improve the situation.

"Ginn, maybe we should leave the ship now."

"How can we use the transporter if there's no air in the transporter room?"

"There are space suits in a locker beside the door to the cargo hold. I saw them when I went on that tour of the ship you were too lazy to take."

Ginnela stood up. "First we'd better see if there's a way into the transporter room. The door from our corridor is sealed off. Let's go up to the crew's quarters. If that door can be opened, then we'll put on suits, open and shut it quickly before too much air escapes, and go to the transporter. We'll have to hold onto the railings tightly so we won't get swept out into hyperspace."

Followed by Lof, who grunted in protest because it was past his nap time, they went back to the dining salon, through the kitchen, up to the crew's corridor, and back toward the transporter room. The end was blocked by another emergency panel, and there was no way to open it.

"Pete, I just thought—what if somebody tries to rescue us by transporting back to the Samson from Merkina! They'll die because there's no air in the transporter room!"

"Come on," said Pete, picking up Lof and leading the way back to the control room. "We'll call them on the hycom and warn them."

"I don't know how to work the hycom. Do you?"

"No. We'll just ask the computer to do it. Wait!" His eyes widened. "Did you say the main computer is out?"

"The bridge computer works. I heard it talk to the Captain. Besides, we still have lights and life support and artificial gravity in this part of the Samson, so things aren't too bad." Ginnela sat down in the Captain's chair.

"Computer, please turn on the hycom for us."

"Unauthorized person giving orders," said the computer, its voice coming from the air of the control room.

"This is an emergency," said Pete. "Turn on hycom."

"Unauthorized person giving orders."

Lof began to howl.

"Shut up, Lof," said Pete, stroking the pink fur until it flattened in the patterns of calmness. "I guess I feel a little like howling, too. Stupid computer."

"Computer," said Ginnela, making her voice as deep and slow as possible. "Who is authorized to give you orders?"

"Official personnel of Fedcargo Samson."

"Scan the ship, computer. Find the official personnel."

There was hardly a pause before the computer answered. "There are no living beings outside the control room."

"Any dead ones?" asked Pete.

"No."

Pete cuddled Lof to his chin. "I'm glad nobody's transported back yet. If anything happened to them it would be my fault. Maybe I didn't fasten Lof's travel case properly."

"Computer," said Ginnela, "if my brother and I are the only living beings on board the Samson, then we are the ship's personnel. I am now Captain Wayd. My brother is First Officer. You must obey our orders."

"Yes, Captain."

"Turn on the hycom."

"Hycom and transporter are devices that send signals and

objects by way of hyperspace from one point in normal space to another. Neither can be operated while the ship itself is in hyperspace, Captain."

Pete smiled. "Then nobody can transport into the airless transporter room and die."

"But we have to use the hycom to let the Federation know we're still alive inside the Samson," said Ginnela. "Computer, take the ship to normal space."

"That is not possible, Captain. One of the drive engines was damaged by the collision. The other drive engine went into overload and exploded."

"But the damaged drive engine must still be working because the Samson reentered hyperspace *after* the explosion."

"The Samson's drive engines are inoperable, Captain."

"But how . . ."

"Captain, I can only make what a human would call a guess, based on minimal data picked up by the scanners in the transporter room before they ceased functioning."

"Okay, guess."

The computer was silent.

"What's the matter, computer?" asked Pete.

"Captain, First Officer Wayd—I am only a small brain, designed with emotive circuits to please control room officers. My tie to the main computer is gone, and I feel inadequate."

"I order you to make a guess," said Ginnela.

"The minimal evidence indicates that it was the other ship that took both itself and the Samson back into hyperspace."

"I thought that ship had cracked open, too," said Ginnela. "Everything in it was escaping, leaking out of the rip in the Samson's hull. Oh, my goodness—I didn't see bodies, but did your scanners pick up any sign of people on that ship?"

"Before the transporter room scanners ceased functioning,

they indicated that the ship is merely a drone cargo ship, run only by computer."

"Then ask that ship's computer to take both ships back to normal space again."

"I cannot do that, Captain. There is now no way to communicate with that ship, and even if there were . . ."

"Well?"

"The brief scanning indicated that the computer is an unknown type, using an unknown language."

"What kind of unknown language?" asked Ginnela. "If it isn't a known computer language, or Federation Standard, then which of the old Terran languages is it?"

"Captain, I cannot use the main library bank with the main computer destroyed. The small encyclopedia in my own memory bank says that the language is not on record."

"An *alien* language?" said Pete. "I thought there were no aliens in our Milky Way galaxy."

"First Officer Wayd, there is no genuine evidence that any intelligent species other than Homo sapiens exists. There are only rumors that on certain planets it appears as if evidence for alien colonization has been carefully erased."

"Be logical, computer," Ginnela said, feeling as if she were hitting it below its figurative belt. "If the language is totally unknown, then it must be an alien ship."

"I do not know, Captain. I will do my best to obey your orders and answer your questions, but my cognitive faculties are limited. I apologize."

"It's all right if you're not very smart, computer," said Pete quickly. "We like you, and we're grateful that you're here, and we think you're doing okay."

"Thank you, First Officer Wayd."

"Can you think of any way of getting us out of hyper-space, computer?" asked Ginnela.

"No, Captain. I apologize."

16

Pete looked at Ginnela and tried to laugh. "Hey, no big deal. Just three of us lost in hyperspace, that's all." He patted Lof, who was making hissing noises.

"Four of us," said the computer.

ENERGY SUPPLY

"Lof's hungry," said Pete. "So am I. Let's go to the kitchen right now."

They went down, Lof trotting ahead this time, his nose swaying from side to side in search of food smells.

The kitchen seemed unusually clean until Ginnela remembered that the passengers had already eaten the last meal on board—breakfast—so there'd been plenty of time before the crash for the crew to clean up. The apple pie must have been baked for the crew's dinner.

"We'll have to be nice to the computer," said Pete, taking some cheese out of the refrigerator. "It doesn't have the main computer to rely on any more. I've read that computers with emotive circuits break down more easily than others."

"I will try not to break down, First Officer Wayd. I will try to keep my emotive circuits under control."

Ginnela laughed, and some of the tightness in her loosened up. "The computer can hear us no matter where we are, Pete. Now, computer, I want to take inventory. Please tell us how much food is left in the Samson."

"There is enough fresh and frozen food to last two humans approximately two or three weeks, depending on how much you eat. You can also use the food synthesizer."

"Let's order a fancy meal from the synthesizer," said Pete. "The food we ate on the trip was dull, and now we can have what we want."

"Can we have a fancy meal, computer?" asked Ginnela.

"What would you like, Captain? I control the food synthesizer."

"Filet of sole almandine, with whipped potatoes and peas, and then the rest of that apple pie on the table."

"And you, First Officer Petevus Wayd?"

"Some of the pie, but first I'll have roast beef and gravy on whipped potatoes and some of the peas."

"I will now start the food synthe—"

"Wait!" shouted Ginnela.

"What's the matter, Ginn?"

"I've remembered something. Mom always said it's important to know about energy—how much there is of it, how long it will last, and where you can get more of it. Computer, what energy is the ship using right now?"

"In hyperspace the ship uses energy from storage cells in the cargo hold."

"How can we recharge the storage cells?"

"The cells cannot be recharged as long as the ship remains in hyperspace, Captain."

Pete, who had been holding the refrigerator open so he could see everything inside, shut the door with a bang.

Ginnela took a deep breath. "Computer, how much stored energy does the Samson have right now?"

"That depends entirely on the use to which it is put. If I

19

explained in mathematical terms it would mean little to you. The food synthesizer, unfortunately, uses a considerable amount of energy. . . ."

"Okay, okay. Tell us how long the energy supply will last if we just ate the fresh and frozen food and didn't use the food synthesizer until we had to?"

"Four weeks, Captain."

"Four *weeks*! What's it being used for?"

"The energy from storage cells is presently used to power the auxiliary motor below the hold. When the main engines are not operating, this motor maintains the ship's protective field, artificial gravity, and the life support system, as well as the functioning of all equipment in the control room, including me."

Pete put a piece of cheese on a roll and handed it to Ginnela. "I guess I won't have a hot meal after all."

Ginnela could not eat. She felt cold all over, and saw that Pete was so pale that his freckles stood out more.

"Computer, can the auxiliary motor be used as a drive engine to take us back to normal space?"

"No, Captain."

"Ginn, we don't need all those cabins, or even the dining salon. Couldn't we save energy, somehow?"

"First Officer Wayd, energy may be saved if life support is shut down to parts of the ship," said the computer. "May I suggest the passenger cabins and the dining salon?"

Ginnela stuffed the cheese into the roll and put the whole thing in the pocket of her tunic. "First we have to collect what we can use. Then I'll tell you what to shut off."

They left Lof in the kitchen, munching on a bowl of lettuce, and Ginnela went up the ramp to the crew's quarters once more.

"Why are we going up here?" asked Pete.

"The passenger cabins won't have anything in them," said

Ginnela. "Everyone was packed and ready to transport to Merkina when the crash happened, and now they've all left. Our luggage was in the transporter room, and I think I saw it go outside the broken hull with the escaping air, along with all those packages from the alien ship."

"But Ginn! I have to have the suitcase!"

"Nothing we can do about it, Pete. Maybe you can manage with the clothes of the smallest crew member. They won't have had time to pack."

His lower lip was trembling. "You don't understand. It's Lof. He can't survive without sulfur pills, and I only have a small packet of them in my pocket—the rest were in the suitcase." He took out the packet and counted them. "Fifteen. I'll have to cut them in half—he won't like it, but then he'll last four weeks, same as us."

"Don't talk that way, Pete! Just because there's only enough energy for four weeks doesn't mean we're going to die then. Besides, we'll make the energy last longer. You'll see."

"But there aren't any sulfur pills for Lof."

"Maybe we'll find some somewhere. Let's look all through the crew's quarters."

They found plenty of clothes and toothpaste and soap and other things to make life pleasanter, but no sulfur pills.

"We'll think of something, Pete. In the meantime, I think we should stay in the Captain's cabin. It's right next to the control room. We'll take one of the mattresses from a crew cabin and put it on the floor for you. Will that be all right?"

"Sure," said Pete gloomily. "Lof likes it better when we're all together."

They moved everything they thought they might need, including books and reading cubes, to the Captain's cabin.

"This is a great cabin," said Ginnela, trying to cheer up Pete. "Look at those old novels about the sea, and the

nautical charts on the walls, and there are plenty of music cubes we can listen to."

"If it doesn't take too much energy."

"First Officer Wayd, the music player takes little energy," said the computer.

"Good," said Ginnela briskly. "Computer, does your encyclopedia say which foods are rich in sulfur?"

"Nuts, cabbage, onions, garlic, asparagus, legumes, eggs, fish, and meat."

Pete's face lit up. "We'll feed him all of those except the fish and meat, which he won't eat. But he likes eggs, and I saw a supply of dried vegetables."

"Is there any food stored in the cargo hold?" asked Ginnela. "Any medical supplies or suitcases?"

"No, Captain. The hold is presently filled with agricultural machinery for Merkina."

"Okay. Computer, shut off life support and artificial gravity to every part of the ship except the Captain's cabin, the kitchen, the corridors, and the control room."

"Done, Captain."

"How long will the stored energy last now?"

"Approximately four months, even if you use the food synthesizer for the last three, Captain."

"What's the use, Ginn? Lof's going to die before that."

"As long as we're alive we'll try to keep Lof alive," said Ginnela. "Computer, I order you to shut off your sensors to this cabin."

"But Captain, if there is an emergency—"

"Just your sensors. Leave the speakers on in case you need to call us—for emergencies only."

After a moment, Ginnela asked, "Computer, are you still listening in this cabin?"

"Captain, my emotive centers are disturbed. This has never happened before. Captain Velsky liked to talk privately to me when he was in *this* cabin, and sometimes we would play games based on techniques developed by Terran ocean ships centuries ago. Don't you want to play games? And what if you need to call *me* in an emergency?"

"Maybe we'll play games in the control room, not here, computer. Leave one auditory sensor set to turn on if either Pete or I yell 'help.' "

"Very well, Captain. Do you want me to leave now?"

"Yes."

"Good-bye, Captain and First Officer. I will await your return to the control room."

There was silence, and then Pete said, "It's lonely. Why did you order it to stop listening to what we say in here?"

Ginnela felt terribly tired. She tried to take a bite of the roll but stopped. "I think we need privacy. This small computer isn't very bright, and it isn't very—well, adult. It's like a kid, lost without its parent, the big computer. You and I will get tired pretending every minute to be its commanding officers."

"You're almost grown up, Ginn, and I won't be a kid much longer, unless I die in four months." Pete held his stomach. "The cheese I ate feels awful inside. I think I'm going to throw it up." He ran hard for the Captain's bathroom.

Ginnela walked to the control room next door. "Computer, I have another question. Will the air in our part of the ship last a while after the life support system dies?"

"Yes, Captain. Biologicals will last until all the oxygen goes if you are careful with your water and food."

"What will happen to you, computer?"

"When the energy supply is drained, I will die."

24

4

NIGHTMARE

In the timelessness of hyperspace, the clocks of Fedcargo Samson showed the hours that were passing in the normal space-time of the universe. The children's biological clocks also told them about time, but there were problems.

Ginnela tried to get Pete's mind off the fact that they were lost in hyperspace. She put him to work turning the Captain's cabin into living quarters for themselves. Pete loved to sleep on a mattress on the floor so Ginnela took one closet and the bunk and put the books she wanted on the Captain's desk. Pete made up his floor bed and put everything he'd collected into another closet, the one where Captain Velsky hung his dress uniform.

"If we manage to stay alive, maybe someday I'll fit the uniform," Pete said, running his finger along the gold braid that even merchant marine captains liked to have.

"Sure," said Ginnela. But she thought to herself, there isn't a hope of that. He's only nine, and we can't last that long in the Samson, not in hyperspace.

They managed to eat a small dinner of left-over chicken,

coleslaw and apple pie, and then, before they thought too much about the fact that they were not having dinner on Merkina with an uncle and aunt, Ginnela said, "I'm tired. We're both tired. Let's go to bed early and tackle the problem of the other ship in the morning."

"I wish it would be a real morning, with a planet turning so the sun seems to come up. I've always liked mornings. Do you think we'll ever see dawn again, Ginn?"

"Of course. We'll be rescued somehow. Let's pretend we're having an adventure."

Pete yawned. "Maybe we are. I just wish it didn't feel so frightening. And lonely."

It took Ginnela much longer than Pete to go to sleep because she kept thinking, over and over, that if the alien ship could take the Samson into hyperspace, it could also take the Samson out of hyperspace. But how could she persuade it?

She had slept only a few hours when she was awakened by a scream. Blearily, she looked over to Pete's mattress, thinking that Lof had decided to make trouble. In the dim night-light of the cabin she saw that Lof was indeed awake, but he was patting Pete's head, and Pete was still asleep.

"No!" shouted Pete, his arms flailing around as if an enemy were after him. He was crying in his sleep, tears shining on his freckled cheeks.

"Lof, are you bothering Pete?" asked Ginnela, knowing perfectly well that loffos were not even as bright as Terran cats. Lof moaned, an indication that he was upset about the condition of his owner. Ginnela hopped out of the bunk.

"Pete, wake up. You must be having a nightmare."

"Ginn! We blew up! We're dying . . ."

"No, Pete. We're okay. You're all right. I'm here."

He clung to her, sobbing. "We're trapped out here. And Mom and Dad died in space!"

27

"That was because their spaceliner blew up. They died very quickly, with no pain at all, I'm sure."

"The Samson's had a space accident, just like them."

"Not that kind, Pete. Just a little collision with another ship. The accident Mom and Dad died in was the worst in a century."

"But one of the Samson's engines did blow up, and maybe the one that's damaged will, or the other ship will blow. . . ."

"I don't think so. It would have done it by now. We'll be all right. We'll get home."

Pete's face crumpled, and he shook his head. "We're orphans. We don't belong to anybody. We haven't had a real home since Mom and Dad died."

"Well, it really wasn't our fault we couldn't get along with our horrible cousins. . . ."

"They said I'm a brat. Am I?"

"Of course not. Only sometimes."

"And they kept calling you bossy."

There was a pause. Ginnela gulped. "I couldn't help being the oldest, and I had to pretend to be a grown-up. I thought Uncle Vin and Aunt Lois would appreciate it."

"You're only a little bossy, Ginn. Besides, I didn't like Aunt Lois. She said they were sending us to Merkina because Uncle Roy and Aunt Della could afford our education, but I know she just wanted to get rid of us. Merkina isn't our home, and we'll never belong anywhere."

"Don't be silly. We're going to have a good time living on Merkina." She hugged Pete and wished she could believe her own words. "Anyway, Uncle Roy even likes loffos."

"But Lof will be dead by the time we get to Merkina, if we ever do get there."

"Maybe not. And Uncle Roy can buy you a new loffo."

"I want Lof. He's my loffo, and we love each other."

28

"Go back to sleep, Pete."

He lay back on the mattress, and Lof, warbling very softly, plastered himself along the left side of Pete's chest. Pete's left arm curled around Lof.

"He likes to listen to my heartbeat," said Pete. "Maybe it makes him feel safe. Maybe I could go back to sleep if you told me a story, Ginn."

"It's so late . . ."

"Please, the way you did when I was six and didn't understand what it meant to be an orphan."

Ginnela looked at the tears drying on his cheeks. Lof's warbling was now almost inaudible, and she could hear the soft hum that meant the ship was still alive. On the cabin walls, the nautical charts glowed faintly, their colors pale but giving the cabin a feeling of homeyness, as if someone lived in it who enjoyed being there.

"Maybe I shouldn't have told the computer to leave this room," said Ginnela. "You could play games with it whenever you couldn't sleep."

"I don't want to play games. They were always playing games at Uncle Vin's, and I hated it. Tell me a story."

"Okay. Once there was a very happy family named Wayd. The mother was a physicist and the father a music teacher, and they had two lovely children who learned many things before the parents—left. They learned so many things that they could manage, the rest of their lives, by themselves."

"What things?" asked Pete drowsily, as he always asked.

This time Ginnela decided to change the story. Pete wasn't so little any more. She tried to remember the important things Mom and Dad had taught her.

"The parents taught the two lovely children that beauty is everywhere, even in the middle of what looks horrible. They said that the best way to manage horrible problems is to get rid of fear and to try to understand what's going on. Then

29

to work as hard as possible, using every bit of brain power you have, to solve the problems. . . ."

"But how can we? We're lost in hyperspace and nobody can find us and rescue us, and we're not all that smart and the computer is so dumb, and we're just kids!" He was wide awake and starting to cry again.

She held his right hand, cold in hers. "Wait, Pete. Mom and Dad used to say you always have a choice in the way you react to horrible problems. You can let yourself be helpless and give up—"

"We *are* helpless!"

"No! We're not. We're alive and . . . and we'll think of some way out of this. Don't be such an idiot. You're not six any more. We've managed for three years without Mom and Dad, and we've learned we can count on ourselves—and each other."

"You're just a kid. Twelve years old."

"A while ago you said I was almost grown up. Well, I've had to be, for a long time. Mom and Dad said that instead of being helpless you could keep on trying, forever, and that's what I'm going to do. We'll get home somehow."

He yawned, wide. "Okay, big grown-up sister, but you know we don't have a real home any more."

Ginnela tucked the blanket around Pete and Lof. "We have lots of homes. Right now we're living in the Samson."

Soon Pete and Lof were asleep, and Ginnela went back to the Captain's bunk. On the wall at the foot was the prettiest nautical chart of all, full of colored flags. She wondered what games Velsky had played with the computer.

"All of normal space-time is home," whispered Ginnela. "And I'm going to get us back there."

5

THE OTHER SHIP

"I'm going over to the other ship," said Ginnela after a breakfast of the scrambled eggs they were using up for themselves and Lof. She led the way to the cargo-hold door, in the corridor off the kitchen. "Maybe the scanners were wrong and the ship really isn't alien. Maybe it will communicate with me."

"I guess the scanners didn't have time to do a good job before they were knocked out," said Pete. "I'll come, too."

"Sorry, Pete. While you were cooking the eggs I looked at the space suits. There's nothing small enough for you. Besides, you should stay here, just in case."

"What do you mean? In case of what?"

She meant in case she died, but she said, "If I succeed in talking to the other ship's computer and it takes us into normal space, you'll have to let the Federation know by hycom at once, so nobody will arrive in our airless transporter room to rescue us. They'll have to send another ship and transfer us to it."

"How?"

"I studied the plan of the Samson that's in the control room. There's a big airlock in the cargo hold, for things that can't be moved by way of the transporter. We can go to a rescue ship through that airlock."

"Very smart, Ginn. I suppose you're planning to go out of that airlock to the broken hull over the transporter room?"

"That's the only way we can possibly get into the transporter room now, and that's where the other ship is."

"But wait, Ginn! Maybe humans can't go across the hull in hyperspace. Maybe you'll die." Pete's voice rose to a squeak.

"Computer, will the ship's protective field protect me from hyperspace?"

"Yes, Captain, but the field is narrower than usual because there is less energy from the auxiliary motor. You will have to crawl on your hands and knees."

"But you may lose your grip and float away or something and not be able to get back to the Samson!" wailed Pete. "Computer, tell Captain Wayd that there's no safe way to crawl over the hull!"

"But there is, First Officer Wayd. Metal handles have been placed so that a human can move from one to another, and the Captain's magnetized boots will cling to the surface of the hull. Just remember the protective field is one meter deep."

"I'll keep low," said Ginnela, putting on the smallest space suit according to instructions that came with the suit and that she'd seen demonstrated at the required safety drill on the first day of the voyage.

"Everything's been sealed up," said Pete. "Maybe the airlock won't open . . ."

32

"It opens manually, First Officer Wayd, as does this door to the cargo hold."

"Pete, you didn't have any objections when you thought you were going with me."

"I don't like being left here alone."

"You've got Lof. And we'll keep in touch by intercom. Can we do that, computer?"

"Yes, Captain, except, of course, in the Captain's cabin."

"I'll stay right here, Ginn. Next to the lockers." He sat down on the floor, Lof in his lap. "I'll hold Lof in case he's curious and wants to get into the cargo hold with you."

Ginnela closed her helmet and opened the door to the cargo hold. It looked as dark as an enormous cave. She laughed, to cheer herself up. "Well, I guess if I freeze in panic while I'm out on the hull, the computer can send a robot cargo handler to help me."

No one answered, and when she turned to look at Pete, his mouth was moving but she heard nothing. Then she remembered that she hadn't switched on the suit's intercom.

"Can a robot cargo handler go with me, computer?"

"No, Captain. Those robots no longer function."

"I'll be better than a robot," said Pete. "Let me go."

"You stay here!" she shouted, and stepped onto the ramp that jutted into the cargo hold from the doorway. She shut the door behind her, took another step, and lost the ramp. She was drifting inside the cave, banging into machinery.

"Computer! Why didn't you remind me you'd turned off the artificial gravity here!" she said, grabbing onto a thick plastic net that surrounded a crate.

"A ship's cargo hold is always null-g. I thought a captain would know that," said the computer.

"Idiot!" muttered Ginnela, pulling herself along the cargo netting. "Does it have to be this dark?"

Lights came on and she saw the airlock. "How do I open it? The instructions are hard to read."

"Stand on the red platform next to the control panel. Push the top button. When the door opens, enter and hold onto the yellow handle inside. After the door shuts, the outer door will open and stay open until you return, closing when you are back inside the airlock, unless someone else uses it in the meantime. Is that clear, Captain?"

"I suppose so," said Ginnela. She opened the airlock and went inside, touching the yellow handle. The inner door shut and the outer one opened. A second later she grabbed the yellow handle and hung on desperately because the air inside the airlock was rushing out, trying to take her with it.

"Computer! You didn't warn me!"

"I am so sorry, Captain. Perhaps you should abort this endeavor. I apologize. I am inadequate. . . ."

"Stop apologizing. We're both inadequate," said Ginnela, a drop of sweat running down her nose inside the helmet, "but I have to try. Where's the first handle, on the way to the cracked part of the hull?"

"There is an arrow labeled 'stern' inside the lock."

"Oh, yes." Ashamed, she felt around on the hull until she found the handle in the direction of the stern. Her heart beating fast, she got a good grip on the handle and slid her suited body out flat on the Samson's hull.

It was terrible. "Computer! I can't see! Has hyperspace blinded me?" She couldn't even see where the airlock door was, and she was afraid to let go of the handle to feel for it.

"Captain," said the computer's voice through the suit's intercom, "I should have explained, but I thought you knew. You are Captain now . . ."

"Explain!"

"The ship's protective field does not prevent the inevitable loss of visual referents in hyperspace, Captain."

"Does that mean nobody can see if they're in hyperspace, even inside this so-called protective field?"

"Yes, Captain. The field merely keeps your—and the ship's—molecular structure intact."

"Oh, fine. I wish I hadn't started this."

"Come back, Ginn," said Pete. "It's too dangerous."

But she had reached out and found the next handle. Remembering the silvery shape of the other ship, Ginnela found herself wanting to get inside it. "I'm going forward. I mean backward. To the stern of this half of the Samson. Don't bug me about how dangerous it is or I'll forget to keep low."

"Good luck, Ginn. Keep telling me what you find so I'll know you're all right."

"I'm fine, Pete. Here I go to the next handle." She gritted her teeth and hauled herself to the next handle, glad that her boots kept her feet firmly on the hull.

She tried to remember to count the number of handles but got mixed up as to whether it was nine or ten before she reached out to find not another handle but the jagged edge of the Samson's torn hull.

Carefully, she held onto the last handle with her left hand and with her right felt around the jaggedness. The opening was much too small for anyone, even Pete, to squeeze through, because the hull of the other ship was now blocking most of the way.

"Blast," said Ginnela.

"What's the matter?" asked Pete and the computer together.

"No way into the transporter room. The hole's not big enough. The other ship's surface is absolutely smooth and—hey, no it isn't!"

Stretching as far as she could from the last handle, she managed to touch an oddly curved, flat something that

jutted out slightly from the smooth hull of the other ship. Maybe it had instructions written beside it, but in hyperspace she could not read them. She decided to let go of the Samson's last handle and hang onto this one.

"Pete, I think maybe this is the fancy doorknob of the other ship, only I can't figure out how to turn it. . . ."

Suddenly it seemed to turn itself, twisting as if it were trying to shake her loose.

"You're not going to get rid of me," said Ginnela. "I'm hanging on until you let me in, you stupid ship that banged into ours and should have known better!"

"Ginn, come back!" yelled Pete.

"I think it's going to open," said Ginnela. "Wow—it's going inward—it's an airlock, all right. . . ." She fell into pitch darkness as the knob seemed to fling her inside. For a moment she couldn't get her breath, and she still couldn't see, but it was *dark* dark, not the gray dark of hyperspace that was like gluey fog reaching into her brain.

"I'm safe inside," she announced. "I just have to find another handle."

No one answered, and before she had a chance to find the way to open the inside door of the airlock, it dilated and she fell into a brightly lit space surrounded by curving blue walls that glittered as if millions of tiny stars were trapped in them.

When she tried to stand up, her whole body felt terribly heavy. "Pete, this ship has artificial gravity stronger than ours." She waited, and then said, "Pete? Computer? Can anyone hear me now that I'm inside?"

There was no answer from Pete or the feeble little control room computer, but she knew her suit receiver was working because she could hear her own footsteps as she walked heavily on the metal floor.

And that meant there was air inside the ship. If all the air had escaped, along with the boxes, she wouldn't be able to hear her footsteps.

She decided to talk as if Pete were listening. For all she knew, he was, and the Samson's computer might be recording her messages. Perhaps she was able to send but not receive on her suit's intercom.

"There's air in here, but since I saw the boxes escape from the hold of this ship, I suppose that when it hit the Samson there was a malfunction and the airlock opened by mistake. Or maybe its computer thought the Samson was a spaceship hangar or something. Anyway, after the cargo was lost into hyperspace, this ship must have closed its airlock and restored the air."

Ginnela paused. "Are you sure nobody can get through to me? Computer, I'd like to know which of these gadgets on my suit tells me how to test the air in here."

There was silence. "You're not listening, are you? I bet nobody can hear me. . . ." She felt faint and sat on the hard metal. "You can hear yourself, Ginn," she said. "You're here and you might as well try."

She opened the faceplate of her helmet, only to close it again as fast as possible when she immediately began to cough. The air was not only impossible to breathe without choking, but it smelled as bad as rotten eggs.

After she stopped coughing, she looked around the empty room, which must be the cargo hold of this ship. It seemed to occupy most of the space inside the ship, which, after all, was small enough to fit inside the Samson's transporter room.

She saw nothing that looked like a door to another room. Perhaps an automated drone ship like this had its computer inside a compartment that was opened only from outside, when the ship was in port.

The lights were on, but there was no faint, reassuring hum

38

like that of the Samson's auxiliary motor. The only noise was her own breathing inside the suit, and the sound of her boots on the floor.

"Sorry, I'm scared. I'm going back." She turned to the airlock. It was closed.

She could discover no way to open it.

CHAPTER

TRAPPED

"Pete! Computer! Can you hear me? Oh, I hope you can, because I'm inside the other ship and I don't know how to open the airlock from inside. There's no handle, just a pattern of dots on the place where a handle ought to be. I've tried pressing them in different sequences, but nothing happens."

Her legs felt so weak from the high artificial gravity and her own fear that she sat down again. Inside the space suit's helmet, her head also felt terribly heavy, and she propped it up with her hands, elbows on her knees. Then she thought.

"It's no use," she whispered. "Pete can't hear me. Nobody can hear me. I'm trapped inside this ship and I can't breathe the air and eventually my suit's air will run out. . . ."

Suddenly the thought of choking to death inside a space suit was so awful that she stood up. "Blast this alien ship! I'm not going to let it kill me!"

She turned right and walked slowly, methodically to the stern of the ship. It wasn't at all far, but it seemed far because it took so much energy to move in the heavy gravity.

The back end of the room, or cargo hold as she thought of it, was circular and flat, with a strange raised pattern on the surface that she hadn't been able to see until she got close.

"Now is this to be used or just looked at?" she wondered, peering at the delicate squiggles that surrounded two small holes in the center. She ran her gloved finger over the squiggles, but when nothing happened she poked at one of the holes. Her forefinger was too large to fit into the hole, so she tried her baby finger. Even with a space glove on, that finger just fit. She pressed in.

Nothing happened. She tried the other hole, with no result. Then she put both baby fingers into both holes at once, and the entire design slid aside.

She had opened a door—but to what? The room inside was small. She could just stand up in it, and turn around, but the rest of the space was filled with iridescent plastic bubbles connected by thin filaments of wire. Each bubble contained sparks of light that, as she watched, slowly changed color and size in a pattern she thought might be regular.

"Hello. Are you a computer?"

The sparks vibrated for a second, but no one answered.

"Is this the control room of this ship?"

Another vibration, but no answer.

Ginnela reached out to touch one of the near bubbles, but found that there was something invisible blocking the way.

"All right, you're protected by a force field or whatever. But you know I'm here and that I don't belong here. If you're the computer that runs this ship, please try to understand me because I will die if you don't open the airlock and let me out. Please, computer."

She went back to the airlock and waited. When nothing happened, she tried pressing the dots again, all at once, but there were fifteen of them and she didn't have that many

41

fingers. She tried using both palms on as many dots as possible, but no matter what she did she couldn't press all of them together.

"Besides, these are dots, not holes. Maybe the computer opens this airlock, and I don't know how to ask it."

She sat down and began talking to the computer, slowly, so that if it were bright enough it might eventually figure out something of what she was trying to say.

Two hours later, hoarse, thirsty, and in need of a bathroom, Ginnela had never felt so alone and helpless. She sat in the open doorway to what she thought was the little ship's computer room, and looked back through the main room that had to be the space for cargo.

There was something in the shadow, far forward, where the nose of the ship narrowed to a point. She hadn't seen it before because she'd assumed the hold was as empty as it looked, and because she was concentrating on getting out. The something was dark, and seemed to be waiting.

When she got up and left the doorway to the computer room, the door shut, but she didn't care. She knew how to open it, and anyway the computer was too alien or too stupid to talk to a human being.

When she got to the nose of the ship and looked down, there was what seemed to be a perfectly ordinary package in brown wrapping paper, about sixty centimeters square.

She picked up the package to look at it closely. It was heavy in the too strong gravity, so she sat down again. She saw that the wrapping paper had split, showing a shiny green box tied with what looked like gold spangled gauze.

The trouble was that the brown wrapping wasn't really paper, and when she took it off the box, she saw that the green box didn't seem to have any lines in it. Perhaps it wasn't a box containing something, but a solid cube that had been gift-wrapped for some reason.

42

She tried to untie the spangled ribbon, but her fingers inside the gloves were too clumsy, and besides, the knots didn't seem like ordinary knots.

Holding the green box, she looked around the cargo space once more and saw no other packages. She felt very tired and was afraid that any minute she was going to be sick. Closing her eyes, she tried to breathe quietly and slowly, the way Dad had taught her when she was younger than Pete.

There was a peculiar humming, scraping sound, and in her helmet she heard her name.

"Ginn! Are you all right? I had to come over because I was worried about you. . . ."

"Pete! Wait in the airlock! Don't come in! Stay there so the door will keep open!"

He was the most ridiculous and beautiful thing Ginnela had ever seen. He stood at the open inner doorway of the airlock with his space suit's arms and legs in a thousand folds.

"I know you told me to stay in the Samson, Ginn, but when so many hours passed and I couldn't hear you. . . ."

"You did right," she said, walking over to him. "That airlock closes by itself and I couldn't figure out any way of opening it from inside here. I was getting pretty scared."

"Somebody give you a present?"

She laughed in relief, and nearly wet her pants. "I've got to get back to the Samson at once."

"Is this ship going to blow up?"

"No, but my bladder might. I've explored this ship, and there's a room at the stern that has a lot of bubbles in it that might be a computer, but that's all I could find, except this package. It must be all that's left of the cargo of this ship. Maybe it's a gift. I want to take it back to the Samson."

He handed her a piece of wire. "Tie the package to your

44

belt so you'll have your hands free to grab the handles. I strung wire from one handle to the next so we won't make any mistakes getting back to the Samson's airlock."

"I'm so glad I have a smart kid brother," said Ginnela.

CHAPTER

THE PACKAGE

When she was safely back in the Captain's cabin, her suit off and her bladder empty, Ginnela began to cry. Pete patted her on the back, and Lof, warbling softly in a minor key, patted her foot, but she went on crying.

"I'm sorry, but I can't seem to stop crying," said Ginnela. "I'm making an idiot of myself."

"You were very brave, Ginn."

"No, I wasn't. I feel like a little girl, missing Mom and Dad so much. I never tell you how much I hate being an orphan because you talk about it all the time, but I do. And now I feel so alone."

"You were just alone over in the alien ship. Now you've got me and Lof for company."

"I know. You saved my life, Pete, but how can I save yours? How can I get us back to Merkina? Maybe Uncle Roy and Aunt Della will like us enough to be good parents, but if we're stuck here we'll have to be our own parents, and I don't feel smart or wise, and I can't teach you what Dad and

Mom could have. If only I were older and not so scared—I didn't want you to know how scared I am. . . ."

"We're scared together then," said Pete. "We don't have any grown-ups around, except the computer. . . ."

"That's a baby, too!" said Ginnela scornfully. "It doesn't know much, and it keeps apologizing."

"Come on, Ginn, stop crying and let's open the package."

They couldn't untie the knots in the spangled ribbon, and when they tried to cut it with the sharpest kitchen knife, the blade just slid off the material.

They carried the package into the control room.

"Computer," said Ginnela, "I order you to study this package and tell us how to open it."

"Yes, Captain." There was a short pause. "I am sorry, Captain. I am inadequate. I can find no way to open this object, if it does open. The scanners left operating in the control room do not penetrate the surface."

"That's impossible," said Pete.

"It's alien," said Ginnela. "Just like that little ship with the weird computer and air humans can't breathe and locks that aren't designed for human hands to open."

Lof bounded onto the package and hissed at Pete.

"He does that a lot," said Pete. "Wants another sulfur pill. I've only given him half a pill today so far. The books on loffo care say you have to be absolutely regular about their sulfur pills, but I didn't realize Lof would start missing his dose so soon."

"Give him another half a pill," said Ginnela, "and tomorrow try two eggs. We'll eat the cheese instead."

Lof gulped down the other half a sulfur pill and relaxed, his front paws tucked under his chest as he sat on the package and began to warble.

Pete laughed. "Silly old loffo. That's his 'I want to be stroked' song. Watch what happens when I don't pet him."

47

Lof's warbling moved up an octave and he added a trill.

"Good Lof," said Pete, tickling him along the spine of his pink fur. "It doesn't take much to make you happy."

Lof wriggled and the trill changed to a bass rumble, enough like a cat's purr to make humans delighted with loffos as pets, especially since the purr went on in complete harmony with the musical warble.

Suddenly Lof stood up on all six legs and leapt off the package, for the spangled ribbon was unwinding fast. As the children stared, the green package gaped open at a seam that had somehow appeared in it.

"Lof opened it. I don't know how, but he did," said Pete.

"I once read a story about a man who opened a magic door by saying magic words to it. Maybe this package reacts to musical notes, like Lof's happy song." Ginnela stroked Lof and added, "But is it safe to open the box?"

"It's open," said Pete. "All we have to do is push the halves of the box apart a little more. . . ."

"Wait—be careful . . ."

Each green half fell back. Inside the box was something Ginnela had never seen before—a smooth, flattened sphere festooned on top with a tight bunch of metal coils and flat things that looked like funny gold leaves, all layered and mashed together.

"Computer, do you know what this is?" asked Ginnela.

"There is no such object described in my encyclopedia, Captain, although, of course, the larger data bank in the main computer could tell you more."

"Only it's destroyed," said Pete. "I wonder what this thing is supposed to *do*."

"Maybe it doesn't do anything," said Ginnela. "Maybe it's just some sort of artwork, meant to look pretty."

Poking at the coils with his finger, Pete said, "Ouch" and drew his hand back. "It stung me."

49

Ginnela looked at his hand. "There's just a faint red mark, no puncture. Maybe you got a small electric shock. I think that we're just supposed to look at it." She picked it up by the smooth base and carried it to an empty shelf near the control room's hycom screen.

"It's not that pretty, all coiled up, with the leaves collapsed. I don't like it," said Pete, sucking his finger.

"Forget about it. I'm hungry."

They avoided the control room for the rest of the day, spending time in the kitchen planning which of the remaining fresh foods would be best for Lof. Even the next day they stayed most of the time in the Captain's cabin, where the computer couldn't ask them if they wanted to play games. Pete finally put it into words that evening when he was getting ready for bed.

"No point in going to the control room, is there, Ginn? The computer is too stupid to help us, and the package from the alien ship is useless. Is this the way orphans feel when there's no hope?"

"Stop talking about being an orphan. I'm sick of it."

Pete got into his bed on the floor and pulled the blanket over his head. A muffled voice came out of it. "I'm sick of you, too."

"Oh, go suffocate if you're going to act like a baby."

Pete said nothing at all while Ginnela got into the Captain's bunk, determined to start reading the space engineering books she'd found at the bottom of one of the bookshelves. Perhaps, she thought, I can learn enough to figure out how to repair the Samson's remaining drive engine.

"Ginn!"

"What's the matter?"

"Where's Lof? He always comes to bed with me."

"Maybe he doesn't like babies, either."

50

Pete threw back the blanket and ran out, barefooted. In another second he called out from next door. "Ginn! Look!"

Afraid that something awful had happened to Lof, Ginnela ran to the control room.

Lof was sitting on the floor below the shelf where she had placed the strange object from the alien package. He was swaying back and forth, warbling more musically than she had ever heard him. And something was singing with him.

She looked up and saw that the alien object had expanded, its coils shaken out like odd limbs of a tree, the leaflike metal parts shimmering as they vibrated. The music that harmonized with Lof's warble was coming from the object.

"It's beautiful, Ginn!"

"Lots of modern metal sculpture moves with light and sound. I don't know if any of it can harmonize like this."

"Captain, my encyclopedia mentions that various forms of modern artwork have computers inside them to make them move and sometimes play music, but there is no record of any that can harmonize with the sounds produced by loffos."

She'd forgotten about the computer. "That's nice, computer. I'm glad you're trying to keep us informed."

"Don't be sarcastic, Ginn," said Pete. "The computer means well."

"I know. I just wish this alien thing was something we could use to get back into the normal universe."

"The universe is everything, Captain," said the computer. "Normal space-time, as humans call it, plus the field of hyperspace that permeates it all and from which reality comes."

"I don't understand that one bit," said Pete.

"I confess that I do not understand it either, First Officer Wayd," said the computer. "But the best human scientists say that it is so."

51

Lof stopped warbling to trot over to Pete and beg for a sulfur pill. The alien object stopped singing, too.

"I can't give you any more today, Lof. You've had your ration, and two eggs. That will have to do."

"I wonder if it would sing with us," said Ginnela, to distract Pete. She cleared her throat and started Pete's favorite song, "Spacers Ahoy." She got all the way through the first verse and had started on the second when the alien object joined in like a combination of high violin and low bassoon.

Pete laughed. "It sounds good, and it sounds funny, too, the way the song's supposed to." He joined Ginnela and the object for the third verse.

It was very late when Ginnela looked at the ship's chronometer. "Past bedtime," she announced. "We can sing some more tomorrow. You'd better bring Lof to the cabin, or the two of them might sing all night."

Pete picked up Lof, who gave his sleepy hum and allowed himself to be carried back to the cabin. "I'm sure that thing was supposed to be a present for some kid. Or some young alien, whatever. I'm going to call it a music toy because that's what it is."

"Perhaps you're right, Pete. Go to sleep."

I guess we can spend our time singing, thought Ginnela, right up until we die.

CHAPTER

8

TAKEOVER

For the next three weeks, Ginnela kept Pete and herself on a strict schedule. They were careful to eat small amounts of the fresh and frozen food, giving Lof what was rich in sulfur. Every morning, Pete studied whatever he wanted from the computer's encyclopedia (he favored the history of space exploration and articles about loffos), while Ginnela tried to understand how the drive engines of spaceships worked.

In the afternoon they exercised and played with the music toy, helped by Lof, who loved to warble along with them.

Pete seemed so happy with the toy and Lof that Ginnela couldn't talk to him about how hopeless she felt. Once when he was taking a nap in the Captain's cabin, she stayed in the control room to talk to the computer.

"Haven't you any information about drive engines?" she asked for the tenth time. "Are you certain you don't?"

"Certain, Captain. All that information was stored in the memory bank of the main computer, to which I had access before the unfortunate accident. My brain is not big enough to contain all that information by itself. I apologize."

"Everything has a computer brain in it these days," said Ginnela. "Look at that music toy—it must have a computer in it, probably in the base."

"That is undoubtedly correct, Captain."

"Well, couldn't you learn to use that computer, to make yourself bigger, to think better. We need a lot of heavy-duty thinking to get the Samson out of this mess."

"I am sorry, Captain, but I have tried to communicate with the music toy's computer. It does not respond to any computer language I possess."

"What did Captain Velsky do when he felt depressed?"

"We played games . . ."

"Besides that."

"He stayed in his cabin and listened to music cubes. There is a large collection of early Terran classical music."

"What did he like best?"

"The Fifth Symphony of Ludwig van Beethoven, December 16, 1770 to March 26, 1827. Captain Velsky said that in the twentieth century, during World War Two, that symphony was played to give people courage and hope that they would be victorious in the end."

"Maybe I'll listen to it," said Ginnela. "I'm not getting anywhere with drive engines."

When Pete came back to the control room with a book of comic opera songs he was going to sing with the music toy, Ginnela went to the Captain's cabin and searched for Beethoven's Fifth Symphony. When she found the cube, there was a paper underneath with thirteen words written on it.

"Music is the beauty, tragedy, and happiness of the universe put into sound," she read.

Then she listened to the cube, and the symphony seemed to give courage and hope to her, too. "I'll find a way to go home," she said, shaking her fist at the brightly colored, old-fashioned nautical charts on the walls.

"Ginn?" Pete was at the door, looking upset.

"I'm not going crazy, Pete. Just talking to give myself some courage."

"That's not why I'm here. I want you to come to the control room. The music toy's sick."

"A toy can't be sick. It's only a little machine."

"It is sick. The leaves are drooping and the coils keep falling down, and it doesn't harmonize well. It makes a lot of discords and sounds awful."

"All right, I'll look at it," said Ginnela, taking her time putting away the music cube.

"Captain!" The computer's voice, at full volume, echoed in the cabin. "Emergency! Help!"

They ran to the control room and found that the alien music toy had plugged itself into a wall socket. Its coils and leaves were bunched together as they had been when the package was first opened.

"What's the matter, computer?" asked Ginnela.

"The alien object is trying to recharge itself, Captain."

"Is that all? Most toys do that when they run down."

"This is not a toy made in the Federation, rechargeable on the kind of electrical current we use, Captain. Its power pack is different, and it is trying to change the Samson's auxiliary motor and, and . . ."

"And what?"

"Please remove it from the socket, Captain. Hurry!"

"Why?" asked Ginnela, but Pete didn't wait. He tried to pull the music toy from the socket and fell back with a yell.

"I got shocked again!"

"Go to the kitchen and see if you can find some rubber gloves, or anything we can use to hold that toy," said Ginnela.

Pete went, and Ginnela said, "Computer, how can this little toy change the Samson's motor?"

56

"By changing me."

"But . . ."

"Captain, hurry!"

Pete came back with a long wooden spoon and one pair of rubber gloves. Ginnela put on the gloves and Pete wielded the spoon, but no matter how they tugged and pried, they couldn't force the music toy away from the wall socket.

"Computer," said Ginnela, "can you communicate with the toy now?"

"I . . . don't . . . know. . . ."

"Try to explain to its computer that I will take the toy back to its own ship, where it can recharge without hurting the Samson."

"Too . . . late . . . change . . . I apolo . . ."

Silence filled the control room, until Lof began to moan. Pete swallowed hard.

"Computer," said Ginnela. "I am the captain. I order you to stay in communication with us. I order you to tell us what to do."

The computer said nothing, but the monitor screen flared with a zigzag of white lines that tangled together and then dissolved into a flat, unchanging gray.

"Computer?" Ginnela put her hand on Pete's shoulder to stop him from crying.

"It's no use, Ginn. The computer's dead, just like Mom and Dad. And they never came back."

"Mom and Dad couldn't come back because they really died, but the computer is a machine, and maybe it isn't dead. It said 'change,' so maybe that's all that happened. The music toy had to change the control room computer in order to tap into the Samson's energy supply and recharge itself."

"But if our computer has changed and can't talk to us, can it still give us life support?"

57

"It's doing it, silly," said Ginnela. "I can hear the air being recirculated, and I'm standing on the floor, so there's still artificial gravity."

"Maybe those things just run automatically, once started, but what if we want to use the food synthesizer? Our fresh and frozen stuff is nearly gone, you know."

Ginnela stared at Pete and walked quickly to the kitchen. He was right. The food synthesizer did not work at all.

"The music toy has killed our computer, and pretty soon it's going to starve us to death," cried Pete.

"It probably doesn't know it's doing that. Let's go back to the control room and try harder to unplug the music toy."

In the control room, the music toy had detached itself from the wall, its coils and leaves expanded.

"It's ready to play more music," said Pete. "Only I don't feel like singing. I wish it had died instead of our computer."

Ginnela sat in the Captain's chair. "Computer, if you're not dead and if you can hear me, please listen. Remember that we are humans in danger, and you are subject to the laws of robotics. You must try to help us."

There was no answer.

LOCKED OUT

The next morning Pete discovered that Lof had eaten all the remaining sulfur pills during the night.

"He's not as restless and whiny as he's been," said Pete, "but tomorrow he'll be worse. I'll feed him the rest of the canned peanuts and dried beans, but after that there's only cereal and dried vegetables for him."

At the end of three days Lof didn't look right. The wobbly nose and oddly vertical eyes were too dry, and his pink fur looked faded and limp. On the fourth day he stopped eating, and on the fifth he was too sick to warble.

"He's dying, Ginn. If only you and I hadn't eaten so many eggs to begin with. The yolks have a lot of sulfur in them, that's why the atmosphere on Loffola smells so bad. The computer's encyclopedia had a short article about the original planet of the loffos. Humans can't breathe the air, but the loffos can breathe ours if they get enough sulfur in their food. . . . Ginn, why are you staring at me with your mouth open like that?"

"Pete, did the article say that Loffola was one of the planets that had traces of an abandoned alien colony on it?"

"Yes, but it said that was hypo . . . hypo . . ."

"Hypothetical."

"Most scientists think the traces were just natural bits of rock from one of the volcano eruptions, although there were some funny bits of metal nobody could identify."

"Pete, I think maybe I can save Lof. I'm going to take him to the alien ship. The air in there smells like rotten eggs. I told you it smelled terrible, but not why. It must have hydrogen sulfide in it. *Sulfur* compounds!"

"Like the air on Loffola. But the ship couldn't be from there because Loffola has no civilization, and nobody's ever thought that loffos were anything but cute little animals."

"But if the aliens who built the ship that's stuck in our transporter room have to breathe sulfurous air, then maybe they once colonized Loffola. Maybe they even tamed the loffos."

"Humans had no trouble taming loffos. Lots of people like them as pets," said Pete, stroking Lof gently.

"And when the aliens left planets they colonized, they always took care that no traces of themselves were left behind," said Ginnela. "I'm going to put on the space suit. Go get all the rest of the food except the last cans of meat and fish. I'll make a sling for Lof out of one of Captain Velsky's undershirts."

With Lof tied to her waist, she got into the space suit, which was so roomy that Lof wasn't squeezed. This time she crawled on the hull with her stomach up off the surface, counting on her boots to keep one end of herself down and her hands the other.

The trip was easy, and this time she took care to swing into the alien airlock instead of letting the handle throw her inside. But when the inner door opened, she sat down on

the doorway so it couldn't close. Quickly, she opened the front of her suit and took out Lof, closing up as fast as she could.

Lof lay on the floor of the alien ship with his eye membranes closed. Ginnela opened the bag of food, put it beside him and waited. He didn't move, but he went on breathing and he didn't cough.

After half an hour, Lof had not stirred. Ginnela found herself staring at the glittery blue wall directly across from the airlock. When she tilted her head back and forth, she thought she could see three shallow depressions in the wall that she hadn't noticed when she went past it to get the package in the bow.

"I have to get a closer look," she said, forgetting that Pete couldn't hear her inside the alien ship. She draped Lof's sling across the threshold of the airlock and stepped into the room, ready to jump back if the inner door started to close. It stayed open, so she walked across to the opposite wall.

Now she could see a faint circle that seemed to be etched into the wall, with two depressions on one side and a third across the circle from them. She pressed each shallow place in turn, but nothing happened.

"I don't have three arms, you idiotic alien ship." With a few contortions, she managed to stretch out and press one with her left hand, and the other two with an elbow and finger tip. At once the circle dilated into a black space.

It's a smaller airlock, she thought. But why? The ship is small to begin with, and run by computer. . . .

"Of course!" she shouted. "Wait till I tell Pete!"

It was so obvious. Why would a small freighter, run by computer, have any air in it at all? Only if biological beings, who had to breathe air, came aboard at times. They wouldn't want to interfere with the loading of cargo—there was no transporter plate—so they'd use this airlock.

Pleased with her reasoning, she looked back to see if Lof was still asleep. He was sitting up with his head in the bag of food, and his fur looked less limp.

"Lof!"

He raised his head, a green shoot of sprouted onion sticking out of his mouth, and gave her a muffled warble. Then he swallowed and went after more food, something he hadn't done for a long time.

Ginnela stood in front of the alien passenger airlock and thought about it. The big airlock, for cargo, right now faced the torn part of the Samson's hull. Since the small airlock was directly opposite, it must face into the Samson's transporter room!

If I sit inside the passenger airlock and let the inner door close and the outer one open, I ought to be able to call Pete on the intercom and let him know Lof is better. Ginnela smiled to herself and squeezed into the airlock.

It was a tight squeeze, and she didn't like it when the inner door shut her into darkness. The aliens, from a higher gravity planet than Earth, might very well be much shorter than humans. Then the outer door opened, right into the Samson's transporter room, as she had expected.

She'd forgotten about the vacuum. There was now no air in the transporter room, so the sulfur-laden air in the airlock rushed out and toward the break in the Samson's hull, carrying Ginnela with it. There was no handle inside the lock, nothing to hold onto except the edges, and they were so smooth she lost her grip.

The smallness of the remaining hole in the Samson's hull saved her from whirling out into the gray gloom of hyperspace. She banged against the broken wall of the transporter room, but fortunately the jagged edges did not tear her suit.

She looked back at the silvery alien ship and saw, in the remaining dim light of the transporter room, that the passenger airlock door had shut fast. She made her way back to it but could find no way to open it from that side. There were no dots to press, no shallow spots or pits, and certainly no handle.

"Pete, can you hear me?"

"Yes, Ginn. Is Lof—"

"He's okay. He's eating now, and breathes the air just fine. I'm in a little trouble."

"What happened?"

"I found a passenger airlock in the alien ship, and when I went out through it, I was in our transporter room, but the door locked behind me. I don't see any way of opening it. There's no handle like the cargo airlock on the other side."

"Can't you just go around to the cargo airlock?"

"I can't. The hole in the Samson's hull is mostly plugged up by the alien ship so it's too small for either of us."

"See if you can open the door into our crew's quarters."

She pushed herself over there, but the door wouldn't open. "It's sealed, Pete. Just as well, because if I opened it or the door to the main corridor or even the hatch to our cargo hold, a lot of our air would escape because they're just doors, not airlocks."

"I'll come over," said Pete. "I'll go into the alien ship and open the passenger airlock for you."

"Oh, oh, no! You won't be able to because the outer door of any airlock won't open when the inner one is open. And I put Lof's sling on the threshold to keep the inner door from closing. I'm locked out and so are you."

She began to cry and Pete said, "Stay cool, Ginn. I think I know what to do."

"Be careful!" She wanted to shout at him that the whole thing was hopeless because he was only nine and she was a very stupid twelve and they were orphans and nobody cared and the universe had abandoned them.

But she stopped crying, and to her surprise she saw their suitcase, wedged up between the alien ship and the broken inside wall. Now Lof could have his sulfur pills.

Except that he didn't need them now, and they couldn't get to Lof any more to feed him and pet him. Ginnela started to cry again.

It seemed an awfully short time before she heard Pete again on the suit's intercom. "Hi, Ginn. Here I am."

His helmeted head was just outside the biggest part of the hole, and his arm stuck through it, waving at her. "I'd already put the space suit on in case you needed me. When you said you were locked out I looked for a metal-burner in the Samson's hold. There was one in a plastic case near the airlock in case the crew had to burn their way out, I suppose. You'd better get out of the way."

Ginnela hauled herself along until she got to the control table of the transporter. She waited there while Pete one-handedly used a gunlike device that melted the metal edges of the hole to make it larger. He climbed through the hole, and they went to look at the alien passenger airlock again.

"You're right, Ginn. I can hardly see the circle of the door, much less any way of opening it. Maybe the aliens spoke to it in order to open it."

"Or sang to it, the way Lof opened the package by singing. But we don't know how to sing whatever code opens this."

"Ginn, Lof's inside. I have to get to him."

"He'll be all right."

"Until his food runs out," said Pete.

"Our food will run out before his, now. Let's go back to the Samson and tackle our own computer again. If we can persuade it to run the food synthesizer, we'll eat and maybe we'll find a way to carry food to Lof."

They went back, but the computer was still silent.

65

SOMETHING IN COMMON

Two days later there was one small can of tuna fish left, and one stale chocolate bar Pete found in the pocket of one of Captain Velsky's old jackets. They saved the tuna fish and split the chocolate bar, nibbling on it in the control room.

"I feel like kicking that music toy," said Ginnela, "but it would just kick back with an electric shock and go on sitting there, waiting for us to make music so it can join in."

"Why can't the Federation send a rescue ship into hyperspace to find us?" asked Pete.

"There's no way to locate a ship traveling in hyperspace since it isn't really there. There aren't any dimensions in hyperspace remember? When I was trying to learn how to repair our engine, I read that a hyperdrive ship's computer takes a fix on the normal space location it wants to go to, and then hyperjumps there, like diving through water to get to the other side of a swimming pool."

"Do you understand that, Ginn?"

"No."

Pete sighed. "I'm not crazy about starving to death."

"I'm not thrilled by it, either."

"Let's try getting through to our computer again."

"We've tried several times a day for a week. I'm fed up. I'm going back to the cabin and play a Beethoven cube."

"What's that one you play so much?"

"Beethoven's Fifth Symphony. It's beautiful, but so is the violin concerto and the quartets and the other symphonies and . . . do you suppose there's something musically special about the Fifth Symphony that made it so significant during Earth's World War Two?"

"I don't know. Play it in here."

Ginnela brought the music cube into the control room and put it into the sound system there. "I wonder if our computer can still hear what we do, or play."

The four opening notes of the Fifth Symphony, simple and brilliant, filled the control room and, as usual, made Ginnela feel less despairing.

They listened to the entire cube, and then Pete tugged at Ginnela's sleeve. He whispered.

"Look at the music toy!"

The shiny coils and leaves were vibrating. Then the smooth base of the toy elevated two centimeters into the air.

"It's floating! It's got miniantigrav!" shouted Pete.

Slowly, the toy moved in the air toward the two children, turning around and around, its upper part shaking. It stopped just in front of Ginnela.

"Silly alien thing!" she said, trying not to seem scared. "I bet it wants me to play the symphony again."

"It's only heard *us* sing before," said Pete. "It hasn't heard a human orchestra, especially one playing Beethoven. Play the music cube again, Ginn."

She did, and this time the alien toy joined in with a sound that was almost like a wordless voice, singing with human music written five centuries before by a man whose language no one in the control room could have understood.

When the music ended, Pete said, "We can't talk to that alien machine, but it likes our music."

Ginnela laughed. "I read once that music is the universal language. . . . Pete! We *are* talking to it!"

"Well then, tell it to change our computer back, so we can order dinner!"

"I can't. It will have to learn our language. Or maybe our computer can use music to communicate with us."

But a day later, with all the food gone, neither of these things had happened. The music toy joined in when human music was played, but it did not talk. The computer remained as silent as before, and the flat gray remained on the monitor.

Ginnela stomped into the control room and planted herself in front of the computer monitor. She shook her fist at it.

"Ginn," said Pete, behind her, "the computer can't help it if it's dead or hopelessly damaged. And look, with all that singing, the music toy ran down again and is recharging itself at the socket. I suppose that will ruin the Samson even more."

"Computer!" Ginnela shouted, "I order you to speak!"

When nothing happened, except a slight trembling of the plugged-in music toy, she put Beethoven's Fifth Symphony back on, loud.

"I'll blow that toy's brains out! I'll twist its little computer mind until it stops bollixing up our ship!"

The symphony was so loud that Ginnela felt it was picking her up, wrapping her in some sort of power she couldn't

68

understand. She sat down in the Captain's chair and waited, while Pete sat in front of her with his eyes closed.

The music ended, and she heard a strange voice, deep and low, speaking a language she had never heard.

"Did the toy say that?" asked Pete.

"No. It was our computer. It's finally speaking to us but in the alien language, I guess." Tears rolled down Ginnela's cheeks. "I'm sorry, Pete. I give up."

"Look at the funny pattern on the monitor."

It was black and white, an eerie pattern of white balls and white lines on a black background.

"What's that?" asked Ginnela.

"I don't know," said Pete.

"Computer, this is your captain speaking. Can you hear me talking to you? I command you to answer."

The pattern on the monitor changed, and the voice said something in the alien language.

"The computer's alien now," said Pete. "It can't speak our language and maybe it can't even understand when we speak."

By the next day the children were very hungry. They drank water and swallowed some vitamin pills they'd found in the captain's bathroom.

"I miss Lof," said Pete. "I want to go back to the alien ship and see if I can get inside somehow."

"No, I forbid it."

"You can't."

"I'm Captain!"

"You're my sister, and I want to go to Lof. . . ."

"Lof is probably better off than we are, and we have to find a way to talk to our computer."

"That's crazy. How are we going to learn that language?"

"I don't know, but there must be a way. Come on, back to the control room."

69

First Ginnela played the symphony all the way through, while the music toy sang and sang. Then she tried to talk to the computer, which now answered, but always in the alien language, with a shifting in the monitor pattern.

"Funny, but sometimes I think the pattern looks familiar," said Pete. "At least it reminds me of something, but what?"

Instantly, the monitor screen changed from black and white to a solid green color that lasted a full minute before it was replaced by the pattern again.

"What does that mean?" asked Ginnela. "Green for chlorophyll? Green for danger?"

There was no answer at all.

"Blast," said Ginnela. "Having no food makes it difficult to think. I'm tired, too. I'm going to take a nap."

"Me, too," said Pete.

She slept badly, dreaming that she was chasing Lof through rooms full of lighted bubbles, shouting, "Talk to me!"

Pete shook her awake. "You're yelling in your sleep."

She was trembling. "I feel so cut off from the universe, locked into my own language, which isn't good enough now."

"But the aliens like human music, at least their toy does, so we have something in common," said Pete.

"Yes, but what good is . . ." Ginnela stopped in midsentence and pointed to the framed nautical chart that was on the wall at the foot of her bunk. "Look at that chart."

"International Communication Signals," Pete read. "That's from before Terrans had colonies away from Earth. I guess Captain Velsky liked these old charts as cabin decorations."

"Look at that green flag, the one in the row of solid color flags at the bottom. The label says that a green flag is the signal for the word 'proceed!' Do you think the computer

70

was trying to tell us that we said something smart and should go ahead with it?"

"What did we say?"

"It was what you said, Pete. The black and white pattern reminded you of something."

"But I don't know what. . . . Ginn! Captain Velsky and the computer played games in here. Maybe they used the nautical charts as part of the games." He walked around the cabin, studying each chart he came to. Then he squeaked.

"Here it is!"

Ginnela bounded off the bunk and joined him. "It's a chart called 'International Morse Code.' What does that mean?"

"It must have been an old way of communicating—look, there's a whole alphabet in dots and lines."

Ginnela unhooked the chart from the wall, and they took it into the control room.

"If the pattern on the monitor is in Morse code," said Pete, "we ought to be able to figure out what it says."

"I think it's the Morse alphabet, strung out horizontally," said Ginnela. "The computer must be trying to give us a clue."

The monitor screen changed to green again, and back to a different black and white pattern, very short. Pete spelled it out using the chart of Morse code.

"It doesn't make sense. 'Vllxxo' isn't a Terran word."

"It must be an alien word," said Ginnela, disappointed. "The stupid computer is using Morse for the alien language. That's no help at all."

Suddenly the computer's new deep voice said, "Vllxxo," very clearly, and the pattern on the monitor changed.

"Now it's Terran!" Pete exclaimed, spelling out the Morse letters. "It says 'learn.' Vllxxo must mean the Terran word learn. That's what the computer wants us to do."

"Great," said Ginnela. "By the time we've starved to death we'll have learned a few alien words. What good will that do?"

"I thought you were supposed to be my older sister and the captain, and keep our spirits up."

"Sorry, Pete." She looked at the monitor and saw that the pattern had changed again to a simple one of three white balls followed by a white line.

At that moment the music toy spread its leaves out to the maximum and played music that sounded like a miniature orchestra. It was the opening notes of Beethoven's Fifth Symphony.

"Da, da, da, daaaah" sang Ginnela, staring at the Morse code chart. "That's V! V for victory!"

"We haven't won any victory," said Pete.

"We're starting to learn the alien language. The computer can still understand Terran, it just can't speak it. Hey, computer! Can you understand my orders?"

The computer spoke an alien word, but the Morse code on the monitor spelled out "yes."

"Then please, please let the food synthesizer be operated manually. We're starving!"

CHAPTER

VICTORY

"Synthesized food tastes wonderful when you're hungry," said Pete as he finished his roast beef, mashed potatoes and gravy, peas, and chocolate ice cream. "I'm curious about the aliens, but I don't want to eat their food."

Ginnela swallowed the last of her banana fritters. "Computer, can you tell the music toy to open the passenger airlock of the alien ship?"

The computer spoke a simple, one-syllable word that sounded like a musical blip, the same one that went with the Morse for "yes."

"Are we going over there?" asked Pete.

"I am."

"We both are. I want to see Lof. He'll need more food, and even if loffos can live off the water in food for a long time, he'd probably like a drink."

"I'll bring him back to you, Pete. We've got all the sulfur pills from our suitcase, so he'll be okay here."

"Is that why you're going?"

Ginnela leaned back. The food had tasted so marvelous.

73

"I want to see how Lof is, but I want to try to talk to that alien computer. If I can, I'll try to persuade it to take both ships back to normal space."

"We only know the alien words for 'yes' and 'learn' so far. Maybe you should stay here and build up your vocabulary."

"We'll ask the computer. Come on, we have to talk to it in the control room so we can translate what it says from the code it gives us on the monitor."

"Computer," said Ginnela from the Captain's chair. "If I go to the alien ship, is there some way I can talk to the computer there?"

The children paid attention not to the strange words they heard, but to the code on the monitor. It spelled out, "You do not know that language yet, Captain."

"You see, Ginn. You're not ready. You'll have to learn the language of the aliens first."

"Blast. We can't wait for that. I'm going over. Computer, order the music toy to open the alien ship's airlock after I take it there."

There was a full minute of silence, and then the computer said, in Morse, "I have done so, Captain."

"Good computer," said Pete encouragingly. "You're not so little and stupid after all."

"At least it managed to stay partly a human computer, even if it's so messed up that it can't speak Terran. I'm just grateful that the language we use in the Federation still uses the same alphabet that Morse code did."

"And that Captain Velsky played those games with the computer. I bet they played with signal flags and Morse code a lot. It must have taken our computer a long time to sort out its messed up mind in order to think of using the code."

"Yes," said the computer in the alien language and in Morse. "The music helped."

The music toy floated over to Ginnela and let itself down

to the floor again. It hummed a strange tune and rustled its beautiful leaves.

"I suppose that means it's willing," said Pete. "But is it just willing to try when it doesn't know how?"

"Well, why shouldn't it be able to open the airlock? If the lock opens to a spoken word, maybe the little computer in that toy can try lots of words until it gets the right one."

"I'm going over there now," said Pete decisively. "I want to see Lof while you try to talk to the alien ship's computer."

"Computer," said Ginnela, "how did you learn the alien language from the music toy's small computer?"

The computer said, "Mind link."

"Wow!" said Pete. "That's not supposed to be possible!"

"Computer," said Ginnela, so excited that her voice shook, "Can you teach us the alien language by mind link?"

"No, Captain," was spelled out.

"Can the music toy teach us the way it taught you?"

"No way to plug into you, Captain."

"In other words," said Ginnela, "we're not computers so we can't learn from the music toy. Can we learn from the alien ship's computer?"

"No, Captain."

"Are you certain?"

"No, Captain." After a second, the computer added two more words, which translated as "possibly dangerous."

Ginnela and Pete looked at each other. Then they smiled.

"I'm going to take a chance. Do you really want to come with me?" asked Ginnela.

"Sure," said Pete, "only this time I get the smallest space suit."

They floated in the null-g of the transporter room, trying to stay next to the alien ship. Ginnela held up the music toy, attached to her waist by a thick cord they'd found in the Samson's cargo hold.

"Ginn, the music toy won't be able to hear you in space!" said Pete, through the suit's intercom. "We didn't think of that. How can we give it an intercom so it can hear what we say?"

"I'm sure it doesn't understand Terran. We'll have to count on our computer having told it to open the lock."

"But maybe that information isn't stored in its puny brain. If the airlock opens with a word, but there's no air to carry the sound, how will it work even if the toy knows which word to use?"

"Look, Pete."

The music toy bumped against the hull of the alien ship, and now Ginnela could see the faint circle that outlined the closed airlock. The toy's leaves collapsed in on themselves, but one of the coils stuck out against the alien ship.

The coil vibrated, and although the children could hear nothing because there wasn't any air, Ginnela laughed.

"It's making sounds, Pete, picked up as vibrations in the alien ship. Maybe we'll be lucky. . . ."

And at that, the airlock opened.

Lof was ecstatic, leaping all over Pete and Ginnela in spite of the heavy artificial gravity. He looked quite literally in the pink of condition, but his food was almost used up. He warbled happily when Pete gave him some of the peas saved from lunch, and seemed delighted when the music toy promptly warbled, too.

"They can sing together," said Ginnela. "And we're going to sing to the strange computer in the stern."

She opened the door to the computer room, and Pete, who hadn't seen it before, gasped and said, "That's a beautiful machine!"

He stood in the doorway of the computer room, to keep it

open just in case, while Ginnela went inside as far as she could go without touching any of the bubbles.

She sang the opening notes of the Fifth Symphony, and behind her she could hear the music toy automatically begin to play. Followed by Lof, who warbled in harmony, the toy floated past Pete into the computer room, playing the rest of the symphony in its odd but pleasing alien way.

When the music ended, there was utter silence for a moment. Then Lof sniffed and padded back to his bag of food as if to say that music was all very well but friends and food were better. The music toy followed Lof.

"Now what, Ginn?"

"We'll wait. No. First we'll use our vocabulary." She cleared her throat and said, "*Vllxxo.*" She repeated it three times and then added the funny short word the aliens used for "yes," raising her voice like a question mark.

"*Vllxxo.* Learn. *Blli*? Yes?" she said again.

From the depths of the room, perhaps from the heart of the alien computer, two thick wires shot out and wound around each of the children.

"Pete! Get loose! Go back to the Samson. . . ."

"I can't any more than you can, Ginn. I'm caught, too."

The wire encircling Ginnela's body didn't hurt, but then two other, thinner wires snaked out from the middle of the mass of bubbles. The ends of these wires seemed frayed into a dozen sharp points, and Ginnela screamed.

"Go away! You'll puncture our suits and we'll die! We can't breathe your air!"

The pointed wires hung in the air before them, swaying like cobras about to attack.

"Ginn, if we're going to die soon, I just want you to know that I think you did your best to rescue us."

"I made a mistake," she cried. "I should have listened to

you. You're smarter than I am. We should have learned more of the alien language before going into this ship again."

Suddenly the wire hanging in front of Ginnela quivered, and the split end formed into a metal rosette, with the sharp points facing into the center, not toward her head. It moved toward her slowly and plastered itself on her helmet.

"It doesn't hurt," said Pete. She looked back and saw that there was a metal rosette on his helmet, too. He nodded to her and shut his eyes.

"Pete! Stay awake! Don't give in. . . ."

"It's playing music," said Pete, dreamily. "Strange, beautiful music, full of bells and harps."

Then she heard it, too. The sound was coming from the air of the alien ship, into the receivers of her suit. As she listened, almost spellbound, she realized that the sound was also inside her head, as if the rosette attached to her helmet had somehow penetrated her brain.

"Pete, it's not music! The alien computer is talking to us in the same language our computer learned from the music toy. We've got to get loose and go back to the Samson's control room. We must learn more of the language. . . . Pete?"

Pete looked as if he were asleep, having a wonderful dream. Ginnela struggled, but it was like fighting a giant python that had not yet decided to squeeze her to death.

"No—stop. Let me go. *Blli*?"

The alien computer paused, and in the silence Ginnela could hear the blood surging in her own ears.

"*Vllxxo*," said the alien computer. "*Blli*?"

The question was unmistakable. "Yes to what?" asked Ginnela, sweating inside her space suit. "To learning?"

"Ginn," said Pete. "Take a chance."

Again she tried to squirm out of the metal coils, but they only squeezed a little tighter. She could still breathe, but she was afraid that if she tried harder, her suit might be damaged and she would die in the poisonous air.

Pete's eyes opened and he smiled at her. "I'm giving it what it wants. I have said yes. *Blli.*"

"Don't do it, Pete!"

Inside her helmet, the alien computer spoke. "*Vllxxo. Vllxxo. Blli?*"

"Blast you. Wouldn't you know I'd get us into trouble by not even bothering to learn the alien word for no. But okay, if you're just going to teach us, then I'm saying yes."

Ginnela shut her eyes and tried to relax in the coils. "*Blli. Vllxxo. Blli.*"

Suddenly she felt as if she were falling into the fields of the universe itself—all of them, wrapped up together, and unending. The field of normal space, the mysterious fields of consciousness produced by the brains of intelligent beings, and the field of hyperspace that was like the background music for everything else.

And while she was falling, drowning in the universe, she could feel the alien computer inside her mind like a soft hand reaching into every corner.

"No! Stop! I'm afraid." Somehow she stopped herself from the wild falling, and without words she pushed out the alien computer. She was back inside the alien ship, staring at the flickering lights in the bubbles that filled the room.

Now she was terrified, for she felt more alone than she had when the alien computer penetrated her mind. "Pete, please shove the alien computer out of your mind. Please don't leave me alone."

When he didn't speak, she twisted and twisted until her one free arm was facing him. She reached out and just managed to grab his hand. "Please, Pete. Stay human. Don't join the aliens the way our computer did."

80

He seemed to be smiling in his sleep. "I'm okay, Ginn. I just learned the alien language. You'd better learn it, too."

Inside the helmet, his face looked the same, and he sounded the same.

"Are you sure you're all right?" asked Ginnela. "Still my human brother?"

"I think so. Of course, I had to let the alien computer learn, too."

"How?"

"By reading my memories," said Pete.

"I'm not going to let it into my mind for that!"

Pete said a long sentence, all in the alien language, and then he switched to Terran. "If you don't let the alien computer teach you and learn from you, I'll go back to the Samson and talk only to our computer. I won't talk to you at all in Terran, Ginn."

"The alien computer made you say that! You're in its power!" Ginnela began to cry.

Lof bounded into the room and jumped to Ginnela's suited shoulders. He moaned, and the music toy floated in, hovering just before Ginnela's helmet. It sang the opening notes of Beethoven's Fifth Symphony.

The alien computer joined in and played the entire first movement of the symphony. It sounded as if a hundred orchestras were enchanted, giving the music more meaning than it had ever had before.

"Whose victory?" said Ginnela bitterly. "Humans? Or you aliens?"

"It thought we were enemies," said Pete, "but now it knows that we have beautiful music, too. And that loffos like us. Please let it teach you and learn from you, Ginn, so that you can give it orders. You're the only captain around, and it says it needs one."

"It had the power to take the Samson into hyperspace, so why is it pretending it needs a captain?"

"It crashed into the Samson by mistake," said Pete patiently. "The Samson was starting the jump out of hyperspace and took the alien ship with it. The alien computer went back into hyperspace to continue its journey, but found itself trapped inside the Samson, with no way of asking its biological masters for new orders. Be its captain, Ginn."

"Do you mean that you want me to order this alien monster of a computer to take its ship and the Samson back to normal space so we can all go home? I don't like being the Captain of this ship too, and mind link is a scary way of learning anything."

"I thought it was fun," said Pete, with an ordinary human grin.

Ginnela gave in. It *was* fun.

The Federation quickly adjusted to the fact that the universe contained other, and even more intelligent creatures than human beings. Perhaps it was easier because the superior creatures were funny-looking, or because the human diplomats had learned the alien language, or—perhaps because human beings had been feeling lonely.

Humans stopped laughing and began to appreciate the shimmering colors and beautiful voices of aliens who resembled huge, humped caterpillars festooned with seven telescopic arms, each ending in three delicate tentacles. Wise humans said it was unimportant what intelligent beings looked like because there is a kinship of intelligence, and the universe needs all the talents that arise in it.

Ginnela and Pete settled into life on Merkina. Uncle Roy did like loffos, and Aunt Della said she thought she could learn to appreciate Lof.

School was much easier than Ginnela expected, and she

earned extra money tutoring people in the new language. Pete started to work on making his own bubble computer, but Ginnela studied music.

Sometimes she sang to herself, deep in her mind.

"I'm still human," she sang, and wondered if it were completely true. One day she asked Pete. "Do you think we're still human?"

"Doesn't matter," said Pete.

"Why not?"

"Because it doesn't. And whether we're human or not, we're not orphans."

"Because of Aunt Della and Uncle Roy?"

"No, because we know we can take care of ourselves."

Ginnela thought about it. "Yes, but it's more than that, Pete. It's because we belong to the universe."

"Like music," said Pete.

Date Due

APR. 1 0			
MAY 1			
MAY 1			
APR 15 '91			
MAY 14 '91			
JAN 9 '92			
MAR 12 '92			
APR 27 '92			